Irma's Wish

Molly Basil Smith

For my goblins:

Astrid, Isaac and Lucas.

It is an honour to be your mummy.

This is Irma.

Irma is a goblin.

Irma is an IMPATIENT goblin.

One week ago, the postal pigeon brought an invitation for Irma.

Irma opened the glittery, golden envelope and a handful of huge, soft magnolia petals tumbled into her lap.

There was shiny, gold writing on the very biggest petal.

Granny Flora peeked over Irma's shoulder and read aloud:

You are invited to tea and stargazing.
December 15th
Lapland

The petal felt cool and silky soft.

It smelled of sandalwood and rose water. It smelled of Irma's mummy, Jac, who had been away at work since March.

Irma turned the petal over so Granny Flora could read the rest of the invitation.

It said:

Warmest wishes,

See you Santa
soon, Mummy
x x x

Mummy! They were going to the North Pole to see Mummy!

They were going to see Santa too, which was exciting, but Irma hadn't seen her mummy since March. Going to see Mummy was actually

THE MOST EXCITING THING EVER.

Ever.

Granny Flora knitted new stripey ear socks, mittens and an extra long, extra snuggly, scarf for Irma.

Chick wasn't used to the cold, so Flora made him a lovely wooly travel coop too.

They would all be toasty and warm at the North Pole.

On the morning of the 15th, Irma hung out fresh fat balls for her bird friends. Grandpa Atticus (well, his ghost) held her legs steady so she could reach the end of the branches.

Just before noon, Granny Flora came to their door and called out:

"IRMA! FIVE MINUTES!"

And then:

"Come and get your woolies on!"

At twelve o'clock precisely, their old wooden door vanished.

In its place stood an archway, made from blocks of sparkling ice. Instead of a door, the arch was hung with a curtain spun from snowflakes and shimmering, magical light.

The three travellers stepped through the curtain...

... into deep, crunchy, COLD snow!

It was so cold that Irma and Granny Flora both yelped and danced in shock. Chick was very glad Granny Flora didn't drop him!

Suddenly Irma found herself being lifted up, flying through the air, into a tight, warm hug.

A hug that smelled of rose water and sandalwood.

"Mummy!"

Irma wasn't the only one who had missed her mummy. Granny Flora gathered them both up into a long, squashy, snuggly hug.

After a while Jac said: "Come on, we don't want to keep Santa waiting!"

The three goblins, and their chicken, walked down a hard, crunchy path that had been dug out of the snow.

It led to a little wooden house, buried in snow and surrounded by trees. White smoke curled from the chimney and drifted into the sky.

Jac leaned down so that Irma
could reach over her shoulder and
knock on the door.

"COME IN!" a voice called from inside.

So, in they went.

There he was, Santa, sat on a low, wooden stool by the cosy log fire.

Irma thought he was huge, for a goblin, with rosy cheeks and a big fluffy beard. He was holding something carefully in his stout arms.

"Hello Irma! How lovely to meet you at last."

Irma was curious to see what Santa was holding but first, Granny Flora and Jac had to peel Irma out of her outside clothes.

Irma felt like a banana.

Freshly peeled, Irma galloped across the room to peek over Santa's arm. Irma gasped and squealed and danced with excitement.

Santa was holding a baby! A sleepy, wriggly, squashy baby!

Jac told Irma that the baby's name was Leif, and that Leif didn't have a mummy of his own.

Jac said that wouldn't it be wonderful if he could have a mummy, a granny and the best big sister ever?

Irma wasn't sure if she wanted to share her mummy with a baby. She already shared her mummy with the whole world for most of the year. Irma wanted Jac all to herself.

But Jac had plopped Irma in a chair and laid baby Leif in her lap. He opened his eyes, waved his fat fists around, then let out an ENORMOUS burp.

Irma squealed and laughed with delight. Even Chick, who was never fond of new people, clucked over the baby with approval.

"My baby."

Santa soon called them all to the table for tea and treats. Irma had never seen so many different treats in one place!

"A celebration! " Santa announced in his jolliest voice. "May this goblin family be happy and healthy together!"

"Wonderful!" Granny Flora said. "Shall I pour the tea?"

Irma bit the head off every single gingerbread man on the table.

Chick pecked at the honey cakes with great glee and picked the crumbs off Santa's collar.

Leif sat on his new mummy's lap, babbling and laughing at his silly big sister blowing bubbles in her milk.

Leif was a very happy baby.

After tea, the goblins wrapped up
warm and sat together, out in the
snow, to watch the night sky.

When a shooting star zipped through the tumbling aurora, Irma didn't make a wish. She couldn't think of a single thing to wish for.

Irma was a very happy goblin.

Keep up to date with Irma's adventures
on Instagram – @irmathegoblin

This is St Luke's Church in Brierfield, Lancashire. They tell you that small door is just the entrance to the bell tower but it is a LIE carefully crafted by the church wardens to protect Irma and her family.

That door is Irma's door, and this is one of my visits to observe her. It is also the day I found out how painful being viciously pecked by a protective chick is.

Approach this door with caution, and bring bakewell tarts.

Printed in Great Britain
by Amazon

72988025R00017